diary of 6th grade ninja 2
pirate invasion

BY **MARCUS EMERSON**
AND NOAH CHILD,
WITH SAL HUNTER

ILLUSTRATED BY DAVID LEE

EMERSON PUBLISHING HOUSE

For my wife,
who hates it when I talk like a pirate…

My name is Chase Cooper and since this is my second diary (my dad *still* insists I call it a chronicle), I'll fill you in on what's happened in the last month, but first a little bit about myself.

Here's my self-portrait. Ladies, please remain calm.

ME.→
HANDSOME,
RIGHT?

I'm still eleven years old and still a scrawny dude. As much as I want to say being a ninja bulked me up a bunch, it hasn't, but that's a good thing since a beefy ninja would be weird looking.

Buchanan School has been good to me. I was the new kid at the start of the year, but nobody really gave me gruff about it. Cool kids and sports stars fill the hallways between classes, and I do my best to stay off everyone's radar.

I'm what some people might call a "comic book nerd," but I prefer the term "aficionado," which means I'm more of an *expert* in comics and less of a *nerd*. It's a term I learned from my cousin, Zoe. She's the coolest cousin in the world, but don't tell her I said that.

I've become better friends with Brayden, the werewolf hunter, but I wouldn't say we're "best friends." We've hung out a couple times outside of school to watch bad horror movies and make fun of them. Trust me when I say it's a lot more fun than it sounds. Zoe came over once and even *she* laughed a couple times.

About a month has passed since I finished my first ~~diary~~ chronicle. If you remember, Wyatt was busted for the theft of all the money raised for the food drive. Since he confessed, there wasn't any reason for the teachers to do any more investigating so the secret ninja clan is safe and still *secret*. You'll also be happy to hear that Wyatt was expelled from Buchanan. I don't know exactly which school he's at right now, and frankly, I don't give a spew about it.

Oh, and all that has led me up to this point, but you've probably figured it out by now. I'm *still* a ninja, but I'm also the new *leader* of the ninja clan.

ME →
AGAIN.

DOUBLE
HANDSOME.

I fought it at first for a couple of reasons. One – it was *because* of the ninja clan that I got my butt handed to me during the first week of school. And two – I was only a ninja for less than a week so how was I supposed to lead an entire clan without any ninjutsu experience? In the end, Zoe convinced me that I shouldn't let the opportunity go, and I finally agreed with her.

Brayden had begged me to let him into the clan, but

since I was a new leader, I didn't want it to seem like I was in it just so my friends could join. I told him no, and that he'd have to wait a few months. He wasn't too happy with the decision.

I also agreed to become the leader because the day Wyatt was busted, one of the ninjas approached me and said Buchanan School was in danger of a pirate invasion.

I know, right? Pirates invading a school? I thought it was just a joke… as it turns out, it *wasn't*.

The whole thing can be traced back to early Monday morning in homeroom. How can I remember exactly when it started? Because it was the most *annoying* thing in the world. It was "Talk Like A Pirate Morning."

"Arrrrrr, mateys!" Brayden said as he entered the room.

I remember sighing the moment I heard him. "Please," I said as I shut my eyes. "Not you too."

"Lighten up," Zoe said, turning around in her seat to face me. "Just 'cause you hate pirates doesn't mean you have to ruin it for the rest of us. Besides, it's just for the morning. It'll stop *after* homeroom."

"It's not that I hate pirates," I said. "It's that I hate people *talking* like them, but y'know what? It's not even *that* really. It's more that people are *acting* in the middle of school and not even *good* acting! They're all just going around yelling, 'Arrrr, matey!'"

"Acting?" Brayden asked. "You mean like in drama club or something?"

4

"Yeah," I said. "It's *super* annoying."

Zoe curled her lip. "How 'bout you keep it to yourself then?" She lowered her voice and whispered. "It's not like anyone is making fun of you for dressing in black pajamas during gym class and running around as a ninja."

I shook my head. "Not the same thing."

"I'm sure it's not," Zoe said, nodding her head and giving me a thumbs-up. It was obvious she was mocking me, but she meant it playfully. *"Mister ninja leader."*

I folded my arms. I hated when she called me that,

and she knew it. Being the leader of a ninja clan wasn't easy, and for the past month, I wasn't sure if I was doing a good job of it. Whenever she called me that, I knew the *name* was a joke, but part of me couldn't help but feel like *I* was actually the joke.

Anyways, everywhere I turned, kids were talking like pirates. It was awful, but I couldn't get away from it, so maybe Zoe was right and I should lighten up.

"Sorry," I said to Brayden.

"Cool," he replied. "For a second I thought you were gonna use your awesome nun chuck skills to helicopter out of here. Isn't that what you do? Don't ninjas do that?"

"No," I started to say, but Zoe interrupted me.

"I heard that ninjas can throw an uppercut so fast that it actually travels *backward* in time and punches the *baby* version of the victim!"

"Har har," I said, faking a laugh. "Very funny."

Brayden continued. "I heard that some ninjas just paint themselves black and run around naked because wearing clothes *isn't* hardcore enough. Any truth to that?"

I sighed and sunk down in my seat.

Brayden laughed. "Shiver me timbers! It's only a *joke*, mate!"

My teeth were *grinding* in my mouth, but I forced a smile. Homeroom was only fifteen minutes long, and all I had to do was wait it out.

The clock on the wall ticked to 7:45 a.m. and the

bell rang out, signaling the start of the school day. The homeroom teacher, Mrs. Robinson, leaned back in her chair and started making the announcements for the day.

"*Arrr, mateys!*" said Mrs. Robinson as she cracked a smile and squeezed one eye shut. "Ya scurvy sailors can call me 'One Eyed Robinson!'"

The entire room full of students responded, shouting, "*Arrrrrr!*"

It would've made me angry if it weren't actually funny. I LOL'd, but so did the rest of the students.

"Here be the announcements, ya scallywags!" Mrs. Robinson continued. She was younger than most teachers and by far the prettiest one at the school. And by *pretty*, I mean she wasn't so old that her face looked like it was trying to run away from her skull. "*Firstly*, I must thank the lot of ya for joinin' me in this wonderful celebration of talkin' like a pirate!"

Several students grumbled in response. I think they were saying, "You're welcome," in their own pirate way. I don't think grammar was too important to them.

"*Secondably*," Mrs. Robinson said, confirming the bit about grammar I just mentioned. "At the end of the week, thar be the event, 'Dance 'Til Ya Drop,' in which all ye students be required to participate in."

It seems Buchanan School hosts an event every month. Last month, it was the food drive. This month, it's an event to raise awareness of cardiovascular diseases and also to help students live healthier lives. It's called "Dance 'Til Ya Drop," and the point is to get adults to

7

pledge a certain amount of money for the amount of time you promised to dance for. The whole thing was going to be two hours long so the idea was to dance the entire two hours anyhow, or at least until you dropped.

"The school will host an assembly at the end of the day on Friday," said Mrs. Robinson. "Then the *official* event be held at five o'clock *sharrrrrp*. The nighttime event be mandatory. Lest ye have an excuse from yer parents, I expect t'see ya thar!"

"Are you going?" I asked Zoe.

She turned in her desk. "Aye, matey. Aren't you?"

I sighed. "If there were any way I could get out of it, I would."

"It'll be fun," said Zoe.

Mrs. Robinson continued talking. "Remember, there be a prize awarded to the student who brings in the most money – a trip fer yer family to Hawaii, and the opportunity to *change* the Buchanan School mascot!"

That's right. A trip to Hawaii *and* permission to switch the mascot from a wildcat to whatever the winner wanted. Buchanan's had the same mascot for a billion years, and the school was planning on changing it anyway so I guess they figured making it a prize would get kids to try harder in raising money. They were right.

Mrs. Robinson droned on with a bunch of other announcements nobody really cared about - pizza for lunch, something about graffiti in the boy's bathroom, and stuff about issuing library cards.

Zoe shook her head. She turned around and started

8

whispering. "Seems like a mistake to put the fate of our mascot in the hands of a 6th grader."

"I don't know," Brayden said. "I think it's really cool of them. If I win it, I'm gonna make it an alien. Could you imagine that? The Buchanan Aliens?"

"Yep. Mistake," Zoe said. "*Matey.*"

I rolled my eyes.

Zoe must've noticed because she chuckled at me. "Don't look so stressed. This whole thing might be annoying, but it's all in good fun."

"Sure," I said. "My own cousin has betrayed me… speaking like a *pirate* when she *knows* I hate it."

Jabbing me in the shoulder, she spoke again, softer this time. "You know I've got your back no matter what. Even if it means going deep undercover someday, I'll always side with you."

I nodded, glancing at the clock, hoping it was time to dismiss so we could be done with the pirate shenanigans. Thank the stars because it *was* time to dismiss.

Mrs. Robinson shuffled a few sheet of papers, making sure she had all the announcements, um… *announced*. Finally she smiled and looked up from her notes. "Avast! It be time t'part ways!"

Everyone let out one last, "*Arrrrrr*," and then started filtering through the door and into the hallway. My next period was art class, which I shared with Zoe and Brayden. Buchanan allowed the sixth graders to set their school schedules to be similar to middle school.

9

They say it allows the transition into seventh grade to be smoother and less traumatic, but I have my doubts about that.

Monday. 8:15 AM. Art class.

When I arrived to art class, I found that Zoe and Brayden were already there and talking to a new student. The kid was sitting in the desk next to Zoe, which happened to be my desk, but since I'm such a cool guy, I didn't say anything.

"Just so you know," I said. "That's my seat."

Okay, maybe I said a *little* something.

"Sorry, mate," said the new kid as he lifted his book bag off the floor. "But don't ye know that nothing's sacred in a pirate *invasion?*"

I put my hand out, gesturing for him to stop speaking. It looked like I was telling him I knew what he was saying, but really I was only trying to get him to shut his pirate mouth. The art desks were arranged in clumps of four, and the two directly across from him were empty so I took a seat in one of those. The sixth graders didn't

11

have assigned seats anyways so it's not like I could've done anything. "Nobody sits over here. You can have that desk."

The new kid smiled. "Thank ye, kind sir."

I raised my eyebrows. "But only if you stop talking like a pirate."

Just then, Mr. Richardson entered the room and let out a shout. "Arrrr, mateys!"

Great, I thought. Apparently the art teacher didn't get the memo about how talking like a pirate was supposed to be *only* during homeroom. The entire class erupted in laughter and replied to him in the same way.

"Seems we have a new student joinin' us today," Mr. Richardson said. "Everybody welcome Carlyle."

CARLYLE.

Zoe turned to face the new kid. "Cool name."

"I have my parents to thank for that," Carlyle said.

This made Zoe giggle in a weird way. I also noticed that her eyelashes fluttered. Gross. My cousin just fell in *crush* at first sight.

I didn't want to be rude to Carlyle since I was pretty new at the school myself, but honestly I was happy that I wasn't the *newest* kid anymore. I leaned forward in my desk. "It's nice to meet you, Carlyle. My name's Chase."

The new kid stared at me for a moment. The awkward silence was definitely *awkward*. Finally, his lips cracked a smirk. "Ahoy, Chase. Pleasure to make yer acquaintance."

I tightened a smile and ignored the way he spoke. Luckily it was Brayden that said something.

"Oh, that whole pirate thing was just for homeroom," said Brayden.

Zoe jumped to Carlyle's defense. "So what if he wants to keep it going? I think it's pretty cool if he did. Besides, Richardson spoke like that when he walked into the room. Maybe it should be the entire *day*."

Brayden raised his hands in surrender. "You're right. Nothing wrong with that."

Carlyle slowly turned toward me and spoke. "Do ya mind, matey? If I were to speak to ya in pirate tongue?"

It took all my strength to look at him and not laugh. "Not at all. It's a free country."

13

Monday. 10:30 AM. Gym class.

To be honest, the rest of art class wasn't horrible. For being the new kid, Carlyle seemed like a stand up guy. He hit it off instantly with most of the others in class with the way he continued to speak like a pirate. Part of me was impressed that a new kid at a new school would have the guts to do something so odd on his first day. He even made a few jokes that made me laugh.

So all that to say I didn't mind seeing him in the same gym class as Zoe, Brayden, and I. Obviously Zoe was a little more excited than I was.

Brayden and I had already changed into our gym clothes and were waiting out on the basketball court for the other students and the gym teacher, Mr. Cooper, to arrive.

When Carlyle walked out of the locker room, he joined us, probably since we just had art class together and we were the only kids he knew.

"OMG!" cried Zoe as she exited the girl's locker room. "I can't believe you're in *this* class too!"

Carlyle nodded. "Aye."

ZOE

"Well that's just..." Zoe said with a twinkle in her eye. "That's just *somethin'*, ain't it?"

When the rest of the students were standing on the gymnasium floor, Mr. Cooper started making the rounds, checking off names from the attendance list. After he checked my name off, he looked at Carlyle.

"New kid, huh?" Mr. Cooper said without looking

up from his clipboard. "Carlyle's your name?"

"And plunderin's me game," Carlyle said.

Mr. Cooper's face didn't move. "Nice," he said with no emotion, scratching a checkmark on his clipboard. Then he looked up and spoke loudly. "Same as before, children - basketball in here, soccer out in the field, and laps around the track for the unmotivated. For anyone interested, there's some sort of obstacle course out there, or whatever... I don't care. Do what you feel like."

It was pretty obvious that Mr. Cooper didn't love his job.

I started walking swiftly to the gym doors, but slowed down once I realized Brayden and Zoe weren't keeping up. They were lagging behind, talking to Carlyle.

"So where did you move here from?" Zoe asked.

Carlyle scratched the back of his head. "Oh no, my family didn't move or anything. I open enrolled so I could attend here. I heard some pretty nice things about you guys."

"Like what?" I asked, happy that Carlyle had stopped the pirate nonsense.

"Like the way Buchanan allows sixth graders more freedom than other schools."

"What school did you come from?" Brayden asked.

"Williams," Carlyle replied.

Brayden gasped quietly. "That's where Wyatt was shipped off to."

So that's where he was forced to go, I thought. "I

guess it's lucky that Carlyle got out of there while he could then," I added.

Carlyle paused. "Who's Wyatt?"

Zoe shrugged her shoulders. "No one special. Just a bully who used to go here, but he was expelled after the first week of school."

"Really…" Carlyle said. "For what?"

Zoe started fumbling over some words about theft and a fight. I could tell she wasn't comfortable exposing me as the kid who got beat up, so I saved her the trouble of doing so.

"He beat me up," I said calmly. "Pretty bad too."

Carlyle's eyebrows rose, "Wow."

Zoe came to my defense. "No, it's not that he just beat you up. You stood your ground and *refused* to hit him back. So sure, he mopped the floor with your butt, but you basically *allowed* him to."

"Ah," said Carlyle with a smile. "The hero of Buchanan then. That's what you are."

"*Hero*" wasn't exactly a term I was comfortable with. "My cousin exaggerates."

"She's your cousin?" Carlyle asked surprised.

"Yeah," Zoe said. "And proud of it."

I would've felt embarrassed if I hadn't suddenly stepped into the shadow of the obstacle course that Mr. Cooper had hinted about. Zoe, Brayden, and Carlyle stopped in their tracks behind me, gasping as they looked up.

The obstacle course was enormous. It spanned almost the entire field in the center of the track. In my head, I imagined that it was probably some kind of adult bounce house, but this definitely *wasn't* that.

"Holy moly," Brayden whispered.

I just nodded in silence.

The start of the course was a rope bridge that sprawled over a huge pool of water. Right after the bridge was a rock wall that didn't have any floor beneath it. The kid running the course would have to grab one of the handholds of the wall while swinging from the rope bridge. At the top of the wall was a zip line with handlebars you had to grab.

After that point, it was difficult to see the rest of the course. There were walls among walls blocking the view. It looked like there were spinning pillars scattered throughout it. I saw other pools of water and mud that the runner would have to avoid or worse yet, swim across. At the end of the course, there was a flat open space with barriers scattered throughout. High above the open space was a gun that shot tennis balls the runner had to avoid.

The course was a *monster*.

"Beauty, ain't she?" Mr. Cooper said proudly as he approached us. "Just got her imported from *Norway*. The pamphlet said it was something that the Vikings themselves trained with, but somehow I doubt that. It also says ninety nine percent of students who attempt it can't make it past the first rope bridge."

"What's it doing here?" Carlyle asked. "Will students be running it today?"

Mr. Cooper shook his head. "Oh no, it's not ready by any means, legally I mean, buuuuut...," the gym teacher trailed off as he glanced over his shoulder. "I didn't see nothin'."

"Race ya," Brayden said as he smiled at me.

"How can I possibly say no?" I asked as I started running toward the obstacle course at full speed.

When I reached the rope bridge, I didn't hesitate and started climbing. Grabbing the ropes, I balanced myself and walked as quickly as possible over the pool of water. I wasn't sure how deep it was, but I didn't feel like finding out first hand.

Carefully, I stepped each foot over the other on the thick rope. I wanted to look back and see how far behind Brayden was, but this part of the bridge demanded my full attention. It really didn't matter how far behind he was as long as he was *behind*.

Once I reached the end of the rope, I had to jump across and catch the rock wall that looked a mile away. I took the opportunity to catch my breath and make fun of Brayden, but when I turned around, he wasn't there.

I had to spin in a full circle to see that Brayden was still talking to Carlyle and Zoe outside the obstacle course. That dumb-hole didn't even follow me onto the course!

"Hey!" I shouted. "I'm *winning!*"

Brayden looked over at me, apparently too busy talking with the new kid to realize he was losing the race. Whatever Carlyle was saying to him must've been important because Brayden had folded his arms and was nodding in some sort of understanding. Then I saw the two of them shake hands before Carlyle started walking back toward the school.

Whatever, I thought as I turned around. I was about to dominate this Norwegian obstacle course. I didn't need Brayden tagging along.

With all my strength, I jumped from the rope and reached for the rock wall. I could feel the handhold in my fingers as I stretched my body out. All I had to do was firmly grab the handhold…

But I didn't.

I fell face first into the pool of water underneath me, and all I can remember thinking was, "I'm glad this pool of water was here to break my fall."

When I came up for air, Zoe and Brayden were laughing at me. It was embarrassing.

After I jumped out of the pool, I told them to walk the track without me since I had to dry off, but the truth was that I had a meeting with my ninja clan I had to attend. My wet clothing would have to wait.

About five minutes later, I found my way to the secret passage through the border of the woods at the edge of the school's track. Before I was a ninja, the school had tried throwing away some old lockers, but the ninja clan salvaged them. Now they were used to store all the ninja outfits so they didn't have to wear them under their clothing all day long. I heard they tried that when they first started, but the stench from the outfits was just too foul after about a week.

After slipping into my ninja outfit, I stepped out from the lockers. The entire ninja clan straightened their posture at the sight of me. They punched their open palms and bowed out of respect. I'd been their leader for an entire month, and it still felt weird when they did that.

"That's enough," I said through my black mask as I patted the air in front of me.

"What's on the agenda for today, sir?" one of the ninjas asked me.

"Nothing in particular," I said. "The usual, I guess. Everything seems to be going okay?"

Several of the ninjas nodded at me. A few of them sighed.

I put my arms out and shrugged my shoulders. "Buchanan seems to be doing fine! I mean, if there were any kind of suspicious activity going on, it might be different, but… what did you guys do *before* I was the leader?"

The ninja in front of me answered. "The first week of school was spent sneaking around corridors and stealing all that money and stuff."

"Right," I said. "Which is something we're *not* going to do. What about last year? What'd you guys do?"

"Snuck around corridors mostly," said the ninja. "Stole some things from here and there."

Standing in front of the ninja clan was awful. They all understood that Wyatt was a bully and needed to be removed from leadership, but I felt like I was *also* failing them as their new leader. I know they were *bored*, but I couldn't give the order to *steal* stuff! "Ninjas don't just steal things, you know."

I heard many of the kids sigh, disappointed. A few of them returned to their slouching position while others folded their arms or placed their hands on their hips. The first week I was their leader, they never would've presented themselves in such a way. I hated to even *think* it, but I could feel their respect for me washing away.

"So we continue to train out here?" the ninja in front of me asked. "Like *every single day* for the past *month*?"

I paused, shaking my head. "Yeah. I guess for now, until I can think of something better to do, we'll just continue our training. You guys can make those paper ninja stars too if you want."

"There's no point in practicing ninjutsu if we're never gonna use it," said one of the girl ninjas in the back. "I just wish we knew *what* we were training for."

Under my mask, I whispered. "Me too... me too."

Tuesday. 7:45 AM. Homeroom.

As always, I was the last in the room before the bell rang. Even though there weren't assigned seats, all of the students tried to sit in the same spot every day. The seat behind Zoe was unofficially mine. I dropped my bag on the desk and sat.

"You know you're almost late every day?" Zoe asked.

"Yeah," I said. "Maybe I'll fix that someday."

"Careful, mate," said one of the students next to me, "Or it be Davy Jone's Locker for ya!"

I rolled my eyes. "You know that ended almost twenty four hours ago, right?"

The boy smiled. "There be a black spot on ya, matey."

I glanced down at my shirt, but didn't see what he was talking about.

The boy leaned back in his chair. "Yer days be numbered is alls I'm sayin'."

"Sure," I said, annoyed by the way he was chewing his lips. I thought it best to ignore him so I turned back to Zoe and tapped on her shoulder. "Hey, can I ask you something?"

Zoe spun in her desk, excited that I needed her advice. She set her hand on mine and spoke tenderly. "Of course. You can ask me *anything.*"

I laughed, pulling my hand away from hers. "Weirdo!"

Zoe laughed too. "I know. It took *all* my strength to keep a straight face just now."

I wiped the tear from my eye. "But seriously, I think I need help."

"Oh," she said surprised. "Um, okay. Does this have to do with talking to girls? Because it's actually *much* easier than you're making it. I know you think keeping your eyes closed as you talk makes you look laid back, but it actually just makes you look *creepy.*"

"No!" I said. "It's about my *ninja clan.*"

"Ohhhhh," Zoe sighed. "*Nerd stuff.* I'm still *not* interested in joining, if that's what you're going to ask."

"No, nothing like that. I think that maybe I'm not cut out to be their leader…"

Zoe's brow furrowed. "Go on."

"Those kids are bored with me, and I'm not sure how to liven them up! All we've been doing is training every day."

"Nothing wrong with that."

"No, you're right, but I can tell they all want a little more excitement. And I don't know how to give it to them."

"What'd they do before you were the leader?" Zoe asked.

"Stole stuff and tried framing it on you," I replied.

"Ohhhh, riiiiiight. Yeah, I think it'd be smart if you *didn't* do that kind of stuff again."

"Me too," I said. "I spent most of last night studying up leadership and stuff. It suggested I start with communicating the problem with the group and then hearing them out. Like, ask their opinions and ideas."

"Maybe it's just *me*…," Zoe started saying with one eyebrow raised high, "but a ninja clan that ran like it was some kind of club or something? I think that'd be the lamest most boring ninja clan in the entire *history* of ninja clans."

"That's saying something coming from you."

"I *know*. I love resolving issues and clubs and stuff!"

Zoe made a good point, but it didn't help me feel any better. The ninjas were getting bored, and I was determined to figure out a way they could be useful, even if it meant having lame board meetings and brainstorming sessions. Nothing I was doing felt like it was working anyways, so what could it hurt?

"What do ninjas do?" Zoe asked. "Don't they just sit around, hiding for hours in dark shadows until the target comes around? And then, don't they just go nuts in a blaze of black smoke and burn villages down?"

"Um," I grunted. "We're gonna do this again?"

I turned around and looked at Brayden, expecting a barrage of ninja jokes and insults hurled toward me, but they never came. Instead, he tapped at his desk nervously and tried to smile. His eye even twitched.

Have you ever seen a sixth grader fake a smile? It's a sure sign that something is off.

"What's up?" I asked. "Your eye just did a thing."

Instantly, he rubbed his eyes with his hands. "Yeah, I'm just tired. That's all. I got to bed late last night."

"Oh yeah?" Zoe asked. "Studying up on

werewolves and stuff?"

Glancing at the clock, Brayden nodded. "Sure. That's it. Werewolf stuff."

Brayden was acting so strange that it was just uncomfortable. I decided to leave it at that though. If he still acted weird by gym, then *maybe* I'd say something again.

Hopefully, he didn't.

Tuesday. 10:45 AM. Gym class.

Brayden had acted a little strange for the remainder of homeroom, but by the time art class started, he seemed to be back to normal. When Carlyle started talking to him, he completely chilled out.

Oh, and Carlyle was *still* talking like a pirate. I made sure to look angry and say a couple of quick snips here and there, y'know, all sarcastic like. I'm pretty sure he could tell I wasn't happy about it. Zoe and Brayden were eating it up though.

In fact, by the time we were out on the track, they didn't even notice that I wasn't walking with them. Carlyle was telling funny stories of his old school in his charming pirate language, and Zoe and Brayden were almost hypnotized by it. Seriously, did this kid think he was gonna go the whole school year doing this? What happens when he gets to middle school? High school?

29

College??

The bottom line? It was *eerie*. Carlyle was *eerie*. I just hoped Zoe and Brayden would see it eventually.

When I knew I was alone, I slipped into the wooded area by the track. The ninja clan was waiting, and after all my research the night before, I was actually looking forward to hearing some suggestions from the other ninjas. For the first time in the past month, I felt like things were going to turn around.

Unfortunately, I was in for a big surprise when I showed up for the meeting. After I geared up in my ninja outfit, I walked out, expecting to see the ninjas waiting for me, but that's not exactly what happened. When I stepped out, I saw that half of my ninja clan was *absent*.

The half that *did* show up punched their palms and bowed to me. I bowed back.

"What gives?" I asked. "Was there some kind of assembly or something today?"

The ninjas grumbled and looked nervously at one another, but nobody answered me.

"Come on," I said. "Is there something else going on today that I don't know about?"

A shorter member stepped forward and stared at the ground. "Sir," he said softly. "The others... they've decided it was time for them to..."

He was so quiet it was driving me crazy. "What? *Speak up!* Where's everyone at?"

The ninja looked into my eyes and spoke boldly. "They've decided it was time for them walk away from this, sir! It was time for them to hang up their ninja robes and move onto greener pastures!"

"Greener pastures?"

"It means 'better things.'"

"I *know* what it means," I said, upset. "It's... I guess... I'm a little *shocked* is all."

"Shouldn't be," said one of the ninjas from the back. "This group was getting lame. What else did he think was gonna happen?"

I wanted to shout at that ninja, but I felt like I had been punched in the gut. Half of my ninja clan quit, and all I could do was blame myself. When I looked up, I noticed that the other ninjas were standing and awaiting my orders, but I didn't have any. I looked at each of the remaining members before I noticed that one of the ninjas in the back wasn't wearing his proper ninja robes.

When I squinted, I saw that the ninja was only wearing a black sheet draped over him. "You there," I said. "What's with the cape?"

At that moment, the kid flipped the cape off and jumped through the trees. It wasn't someone I recognized and right before he disappeared, I swear it looked like he was wearing... an *eye patch?*

I didn't waste any time and started sprinting through the wooded area of the ninja hideout. From behind I could hear the other ninjas start following me, but because they were all action junkies, I knew this kid would be dead meat if they caught him.

"No!" I shouted at them. "I'll handle this! Everyone

stay here and keep training!"

When I burst from the trees, I could see that the kid
was running as fast as he could through the grass and
toward the school. He had already passed the Norwegian
obstacle course. The black cape he was shrouded in was
flapping wildly behind him as his fat boots stomped on
the ground. It was clear as day. This kid was dressed like
a pirate, which I would've made fun of, but then I
remembered I was dressed as a ninja.

I started running through the field, ignoring all the
kids who were probably pointing and laughing at me.
From the corner of my eye, I saw Zoe and Brayden
walking along the track, but Carlyle wasn't with them.

As soon as the costumed spy reached the school
building, he entered through one of the doors next to the

cafeteria. I did my best to keep up with him, but it still took me about thirty seconds to make it to the door.

The cafeteria windows were only a few feet away, and I could see that one of the lunches had already started. If I entered through this door in a ninja outfit and someone saw me... it wouldn't be the *worst* thing to happen to me, but it definitely *wouldn't* be *good* for my social life. My street clothes were still sitting in the woods, too far to return to. If I waited much longer, then I risked *losing* the spy.

I decided to "man up" and entered the door.

Inside, the room was dark, but far from quiet. I let the door shut behind me as I found a nice shadowy area to hide in. I was on the stage that was attached to the cafeteria. There was a heavy curtain blocking the students from seeing anything on the stage at the moment. I smiled to myself, happy that the darkness was my friend.

The spy was nowhere to be seen, at least not right away. I could see shadows from the cafeteria moving under the curtain, but I could also see some movement coming from the center of the stage up ahead.

Looking to my left, I saw a thin metal ladder that reached into a dark area above me. Once my eyes adjusted, I could see that there was a catwalk spanning the entire stage area, and with my black ninja robes and low light, it would've been nearly impossible to see me.

When I reached the top of the ladder, I crouched down and walked as quietly as possible over the spot where I saw movement. From up here, I could see everything on the stage. There must've been almost forty kids moving around and working on various things. The noise from the cafeteria was enough that these guys didn't worry about anyone hearing them.

A few of the kids were working on different things in separate corners of the stage. It looked oddly familiar, as if they were training for something. Most of the other kids were gathered near the center of the stage so I crawled out farther to get a glimpse of what they were looking at. The spy that was in my meeting was among them.

The kids were huddled closely and looking at something on the ground, but that wasn't the strangest part. In all the excitement, I guess I didn't realize until that moment that *all* the kids were dressed in pirate uniforms and talking in that *annoying* pirate tongue!

Gross, right? But I also noticed that they each wore some kind of necklace that had a skull embedded into the little pendant on it. Pirates must've gotten them when they joined the club. I wondered if maybe my ninja clan would appreciate something like that.

Then, to my surprise, the group backed away from their spot. Carlyle was at the center of the huddle looking down at a large piece of cloth laid out before him. He started nodding his head and patting the other pirate's shoulders. When Carlyle was far enough away from the cloth, I was able to see it better.

It was a blue rectangle that had the words "Buchanan Buccaneers" sewn into it with yellow fabric. At the center of the rectangle was a drawing of a pirate ship.

"They're making a flag?" I whispered.

The instant I whispered, all of the pirates jumped back and stood on guard. Of course it would be my luck that a whisper would tip them off to the fact that I was up here, but I let out a sigh of relief when I saw that it wasn't *me* that spooked them.

A sliver of light crawled across the floor, and Mr. Cooper leaned through the spot on the curtain that he pushed aside. "Excuse me! What're you kids doing in here?"

Carlyle gestured to the other pirates for them to stand down as he stepped forward. "Mr. Cooper. My apologies, but we're in the middle of rehearsing a play for the school! Why else would we be on this stage dressed in pirate costumes?"

"You're supposed to be out on the track, young man," Mr. Cooper said. "You're in my gym class right now so tell me how you've somehow found your way in *here?*"

"I thought someone told you?" Carlyle asked, flabbergasted. "I mean, they said they were going to tell you that I was needed in here for the next week or so!"

"I hadn't heard anything," said Mr. Cooper. "Don't you worry, son. I'll get to the bottom of this."

"Wait," said Carlyle. "How would you like a small part in the play?"

Mr. Cooper tightened his lips.

"There's an open spot for a blundering idiot," said Carlyle bravely. "All you'd have to do is hang out on stage during a certain scene and yell out some hilarious insults!"

Mr. Cooper stared at Carlyle. I could tell from the look in his eye that Carlyle was *busted.* "So I'd actually have a speaking role?"

What? Was Mr. Cooper actually considering it?

"Absolutely," said Carlyle. "I'll have your script to you tomorrow, sir."

Mr. Cooper nodded, but only once. "Tomorrow."

I couldn't believe what I was seeing! Carlyle had built a gang of pirates who were doing something that was at least *questionable,* and Mr. Cooper had just given them a nod of approval! This was insane!

I was going to have to confront Carlyle on my own, but I would need help from my ninja clan. When I climbed down from the ladder, I snuck over to the side door I had snuck through.

"Hey," said a voice from out of nowhere.

My heart dropped as I turned around. Suddenly, there was a bright flash of light in my eyes. As I reached my hands up, I heard the door click open behind me, and then I felt someone push against my chest until I was outside the school and on my butt in the gravel.

Wednesday. 7:45 AM. Homeroom.

Nice cliffhanger back there, huh? I thought it was more exciting to end the diary entry at that spot because the stuff that happened afterward was boring. All I did was dust myself off, change back into my street clothes, and spend the rest of the day wondering who it was that pushed me out the door. I didn't get a look at the kid – the door slammed shut and locked before I knew what happened. My face got a little scratched up, but that's about it.

"What's up with your face?" Zoe asked when I took the seat behind her.

I touched the scratches on my cheek. "Nothing. I biffed on my skateboard last night."

"And caught yourself with your face?"

I nodded.

Mrs. Robinson rose from her desk as soon as the

bell rang. "Ahoy, children."

Come on! It was *Wednesday! Two* days after that ridiculous pirate morning! There were a couple of small laughs among the students.

The teacher shrugged her shoulders and continued with the announcements. "As you know, Dance 'Til Ya Drop is scheduled for this Friday night at 5 PM. If you're not staying after school to help on Friday, then have your parents drop you off around 4:30. You'll need some time to sign in. The winner of the event will hopefully be announced that night so be sure to bring *all* of the money you've raised. Once you've turned it in at the front table, you'll proceed to the cafeteria and wait for the event to kick off. *While* students are dancing, a few select teachers will be given the task of counting the money so we *should* know the winner by the time the event is finished."

Zoe turned around. "How much have you raised?"

"Not a lot," I said.

"Did you even try?"

"Not really," I replied. "I went to a couple houses on my street, but nobody opened their door to me. A couple people even turned their lights off and yelled that they weren't home *after* I rang their doorbell."

Zoe chuckled. "I don't think I raised enough to win, but I got a pretty good chunk, I think. My dad took it to his work and got his friends to donate for it."

Remember that her dad was my uncle – brother to *my* dad. "You think Uncle John would do that for me too?"

Zoe's jaw dropped, apparently shocked that I would suggest that.

"It was a *joke*," I said.

"Better be," Zoe said as she started turning back toward the front of the class, but stopped as something caught her eye. She pointed to my book bag. "What's that under your backpack?"

I looked down. There was a rolled up sheet of paper sticking out from beneath my seat. The last time I received an anonymous letter like this, it was when the ninja clan wanted to recruit me. Hopefully, this was just from a girl or something.

"Maybe someone wants to give you cookies and soda again," Zoe said with a smirk.

I reached under the bag and pulled the paper out. "Weird," I said. "This paper is really old and crusty, and look at this... there's a wax seal holding it shut."

Zoe's eyes widened. "Pirates..."

I peeled away the wax seal and opened the sheet of parchment. *Please be from a girl,* I hoped. It definitely wasn't.

Salutations Chase,
Be in the boy's locker room during gym class today or suffer the consequences.
The Captain.

"Why are all your notes from boys?" Zoe joked.

I took a breath. "I can't *wait* until I actually get a real note from a girl."

Wednesday. 10:40 AM. Gym class.

It wasn't easy for me to stay in the locker room. All the other students dressed and left the room already. Mr. Cooper was always the last one out precisely *because* of stragglers who tried to hide until class started so they could skip. I figured out a foolproof way of remaining in the room though.

"Chase?" Mr. Cooper asked. "You okay in there?"

I groaned in the locked bathroom stall. "I'm not feeling so good, coach. I think I caught a bug or something."

"That's fine, son," said the coach. "But you're going to have to see the nurse then. I can't have you sitting in here on your own."

"I know," I said, sitting on the toilet seat. Just to clarify so it's not gross, I had my pants pulled up. I was faking. "But my stomach feels like it's bubbling or something... I'm not sure I can make it there at the

42

moment."

Mr. Cooper sighed from outside the stall.

"Can I just sit here for a minute or two?" I asked with my voice barely above a whisper.

The coach paused before he spoke again. "Sure. Take as long as you need, alright?" he said. "Just don't take *too* long."

"Ten four," I said. "Thanks, coach."

I listened to Mr. Cooper's footsteps echo against the metal and concrete floor of the locker room until I heard the squeaking of the locker room doors open and then slam shut. As soon as I knew he was out of the room, I opened the stall door and started scanning the area.

I was still in my street clothes. I thought that changing into my ninja robes in front of everyone would've been obvious plus the kid who delivered the note already knew I was a ninja... in fact, I don't know why I think it's such a secret. I'm pretty sure *everyone* knows.

I searched each corner of the locker room, but there was nobody else in there. There was a stillness that sent chills down my spine. Every time I peeked around some lockers, my heart stopped, expecting to see pirates, but there was nothing.

And then the locker room doors opened from across the room. I heard the sound of boots clunking on the cold concrete floors as I stood in place, ready to meet with the pirates head on.

Carlyle stepped around the corner and stopped in

place, several feet away from me. Two other pirates, each wearing gigantic dumb looking pirate hats that covered their faces in shadows, accompanied him.

"Ahoy," said Carlyle. "I see the note was delivered to ya successfully."

I wasn't sure how to respond. "*Duh.*"

Carlyle let out a short laugh. "Seems ya found our secret hideout while you were poking your nose around where it shouldn't have been."

"I only followed the spy you sent to *my* hideout," I said coldly.

"Right," Carlyle said. "But it still doesn't change the fact that you were where ya weren't supposed to be. And that means ya *saw* stuff ya weren't supposed to *see*."

I nodded and narrowed my eyes. "Uh yeah. Again, I only ended up there because *you* sent a spy into my clan."

The pirates behind Carlyle stepped forward aggressively, but their captain lifted his hand, signaling them to remain at ease. "Seems we got ourselves quite a conundrum."

"A what?" I asked.

"A *conundrum*," Carlyle repeated. "Too big a word for ya, matey? It means we've got ourselves a *problem*."

"Seems we do," I said. "I don't know what it is that you're planning, but I know that it can't be good."

"So the question begs… *why* ain't you gone to the authorities yet?"

I paused. "I had to build a case. If I went to the teachers and told them a bunch of kids dressed as pirates were running around the school, then they'd probably look at me like I was crazy."

Carlyle bellowed a mighty laugh at that. "Of *course* they would! Especially since you're the kid that runs around in a ninja outfit!" Then his face grew dark and sinister. "This be a fight ya ain't prepared for, mate. Soon I'll have the entire school in the palm of my hands… and you'll be but a fleck of dust blowing in the wind."

This time, I was the one who laughed. "What do you think you're going to do? You're just a kid *dressed* as a pirate! You really think you're going to do something destructive at Buchanan? The last kid that tried that was booted to another school district."

"Leave Wyatt out of this!" Carlyle screamed suddenly, spitting everywhere. "You're the reason he's not at this school anymore, and in this life or the next, *we'll* have our revenge!"

My legs felt numb as I took a step back. I clenched my fists, trying to hide the fact that my hands were shaking. This kid was intimidating, that's for sure, and I was afraid of him. "What do you mean… *we?*"

Carlyle straightened his posture and wiped the spit off his chin. "You see, you *pathetic ninja*, Wyatt is my *cousin.*"

Suddenly, my head felt dizzy. It was like the room had started spinning.

"When he told me of how you got him expelled from this school," Carlyle said. "I felt sorry for him. When he told me of how you stole his entire ninja clan from him… I promised to avenge him."

I leaned against the cold metal lockers behind me in case I passed out. "What are you saying?"

"Are you daft?" Carlyle asked. "I'm saying that I enrolled at this school so I could get closer to *you.* You've already seen that I've built an army of pirates, and it's only getting bigger. Soon, the pirate invasion will be complete, and Buchanan will be *owned* by pirates."

"That's insane," I growled. "And how exactly is a sixth grader going to take over an entire school like that?"

Carlyle smirked. "You saw the flag we were building, did you not?"

"The Buchanan Buccaneers?" I said, and then it finally hit me. I tried to speak loudly, but my lungs felt empty. "That flag is for the new mascot…"

"Aye, mate," said Carlyle. "I've made sure my

victory is secured for the event on Friday night. My followers at this school have agreed to give *all* their fundraiser money to me so I'd be the one with the most collected. As the winner… I'll have complete control over what the new mascot will be and once it's changed to the Buccaneers… the pirate invasion part of my plan will be complete."

"Pirate invasion part? Is there *another* part?"

"The destruction of you."

I leaned forward and stuck out my chest. "If it's a fight you're looking for—"

Carlyle raised his open palm to me. "Nay. Wyatt's the fighter in the family."

I was confused. "Then… what?"

"It's already started," Carlyle said. "I'll destroy your spirit by taking what's important to you."

"The ninja clan," I whispered.

"Aye," he replied. "Yer ninjas… yer friends… and yer very own cousin."

That was too far. "Leave Zoe out of this!"

One of Carlyle's pirate bodyguards stepped forward. He removed his hat, and turned to face me. I was in shock.

"Brayden?" I whispered.

"Seems he's had a problem joinin' your clan for awhile," Carlyle laughed. "Well, we pirates don't discriminate like that. All are welcome to join here."

"Sorry, matey," said Brayden.

"If it wasn't for Mister Brayden here, then we

wouldn't have known you were sneakin' around above the stage yesterday," said Carlyle.

"You saw me?" I asked my friend.

Carlyle answered for him. "He's the one that pushed ya out the door, but not before snapping a photo of you as proof."

Brayden lowered his gaze. "I didn't know it was you."

Carlyle spoke swiftly. "It still doesn't change the fact that he turned ya in even *after* he saw it was *you* in the photos."

Brayden didn't say anything. My closest friend at Buchanan had betrayed me, and why? Because I wouldn't let him become a ninja? He was wearing the gold pendant with the skull around his neck. The sign of a pirate.

"Brayden," I said.

"Ya got a black mark on ya," said Brayden.

I looked down at my shirt again. Where was this black spot everyone was talking about?

"It means you're marked," Brayden said with a sigh. "That your days are numbered. It's like a giant target."

"Oh," I said as I stared at the floor.

"I'll accept your surrender by Friday," said Carlyle bluntly. "You can deliver it in the form of your silly ninja robe.

"And if I don't?" I asked.

"Then Zoe will have to pay," Brayden said. "They'll make her walk the plank."

"The plank?" I cried out. It was silly to think of such a thing, but then I realized that a pirate invasion was silly too, but here I was in the midst of one. "You'd better—"

The pirate bodyguards stepped in front of Carlyle. This time, the captain allowed it. They forced me against the lockers and held me in place as I watched Carlyle walk toward the exit of the locker room.

"Friday, Chase," said Carlyle without looking back. "I'll expect your ninja robes by Friday, or else it's Zoe that'll pay." He stopped just before the door. "And if ye tell anyone about this meeting, I promise you'll regret it."

The bodyguards let me drop to my feet when their

captain was gone. Brayden didn't look at my eyes the entire time, and I didn't say anything to him. When they left the locker room, there was a silence in the air that felt like it was going to crush my skull.

Why was Zoe always the target for the bad guys?

Thursday. 10:45 AM. Gym class.

It wasn't easy sitting across from Carlyle in art class, but I did it. It sickened me to watch Zoe flirt with him. I wanted to speak out, but was too afraid of what the pirate captain would do. Brayden sat in the clump of desks behind us. He didn't turn around once. In fact, we hadn't said a word to each other all morning.

But that was this morning, and it was time for gym, which also meant it was time to meet with my ninja clan. I knew the remaining members could help me figure out what to do next. Part of me was even excited that I'd be able to give them some excitement for the first time in a month.

I snuck through the entrance at the side of the woods and jogged to the lockers. As I put my gear on, I tried to think of the best way to expose Carlyle and his band of pirates.

During lunch, we could pull the chords to the stage curtain, letting it fall to the floor. Everyone in the cafeteria would see them playing around in their silly costumes, and hopefully they'd make fun of Carlyle so bad that his pirate followers would abandon him.

Or I could go straight to the principal and tell him Carlyle's plan. It would sound insane coming from me, but if I was able to prove he was Wyatt's cousin, I think the principal would at *least* hear me out.

Or the remaining members of my clan and I could confront the pirates and wage an all out war with them. Starting a huge fight wasn't ideal, but at this point, it wasn't out of the question. Maybe a giant fight like that would reveal all of Carlyle's plans.

But it didn't matter. No plan I could think of was going to be worth anything because when I stepped through the foliage, I saw that the secret hideout was completely empty. There wasn't a single other member of my ninja clan waiting.

"Hello?" I said loudly. The only answer came from the wind sifting through the leaves.

Wonderful, I thought. Absolutely wonderful. Just when I thought I could be a good leader, I lose my ninja clan.

If I had been a better leader, no… not a *better* leader. I just needed to be a more *exciting* leader. I just needed to give them a little bit of the adventure they wanted, and now that I *have* it… it's too late.

With nothing left to lose, I made the decision to go

back to the cafeteria. I wasn't okay with sitting in the hideout by myself and pouting so maybe I could have another discussion with Carlyle. I had no idea what I was going to say, but hopefully it would come to me in the moment. After I changed out of my ninja uniform, I folded it neatly and held it under my arm. Normally, I would've stuffed it back into my locker, but I wasn't 100% sure I was going to keep it.

Thursday. 11:20 AM. Gym class.

It says "gym class," but I was obviously running around outside of it. I don't recommend you do the same. You could get in a load of trouble, unless you were trying to stop a huge pirate invasion. I guess in that case, maybe it's alright.

By this time I had snuck back into the stage area of the cafeteria. I didn't step out right away, but instead, I stood by the door. I wasn't sure of what I was waiting for. Maybe there was a part of me that wanted to walk away and fight.

I can't know for sure what I was feeling that moment because a pirate stepped out from the stage and froze in their tracks when they saw me. My heart stopped for half a beat as I waited for him to yell for his pirate buddies. But then I saw that it wasn't a *boy* pirate, but a *girl*.

She stepped backward. Her face was completely covered in shadow so I wasn't sure who it was, and apparently she wasn't keen on letting me find out. She spun around and started running down the side of the stage area.

I didn't know what to do exactly, so I let my instinct take over, and I started chasing after her.

Whoever it was, she was fast – faster than any girl I'd ever raced against at least, which probably isn't saying much since I'm not exactly what you'd call "athletic."

She jumped over boxes in a single leap, even sliding her body against the wall so her landing was smooth. For a second, I thought about trying it, but I knew my legs would betray me so I ran around the boxes.

The other pirates were too busy talking and training with swords to notice that a boy was chasing a girl backstage. The noise of the students eating lunch in the cafeteria made sure that our footsteps weren't heard.

I wanted to shout, but knew that I couldn't unless I wanted a bunch of pirates to chase after me.

She was nearly ten feet away the entire time and her speed was making that gap even farther. My legs were straining from running and dodging obstacles. I knew that if I continued, she'd eventually figure out that all she had to do was run to the middle of the stage to get help from the rest of her pirate buddies.

She glanced back at me and I could see the whites of her eyes. They were afraid and panicked and even looked familiar to me. Too bad she didn't see the stack of wooden boxes directly in front of her.

The moment she hit them, her body flipped into the air like a rag doll, but she miraculously landed on her feet. It wasn't graceful, but it definitely looked like something out of a movie. Reaching for the wall, she steadied herself and took one more look behind her. I noticed a shiny piece of metal drop from her neck.

I started slowing down because I thought she was done for. I was so sure that when she hit those boxes, she'd have to stop running and catch her breath, but I was wrong. She took one look at me as the lights partially lit her face enough that I could recognize her. She turned back and started sprinting down the hallway of the school and out of sight.

I wanted to run after her, but I couldn't. My mouth was so dry from my heavy breathing that I had to stop and find water before I died. But even if I was able to run still, I don't know if I would have. I caught a glimpse of the girl's face. The second it happened, I felt like my brain exploded. It was possible that I was a walking zombie, killed by the shock of what I had just seen.

I glanced at the ground, at a small piece of metal that reflected the fluorescent lights above. It was the piece of metal that dropped from the girl's neck right before she took off again.

I picked it up, inspecting the gold medallion carefully, studying the tiny skull embedded into the surface. It was the mark of being a pirate. The other pirates wore them too. Looking up, I scanned the hallway, exhausted and sad at realizing who it was I had been chasing after…

It was Zoe… and she was a pirate.

PIRATE PENDANT.

MY HAND.

Friday. 7:45 AM. Homeroom.

I made sure I was the first to homeroom. I wanted
to be there to see if Zoe had anything to say for herself,
but after the bell rang, she wasn't in the room. It wasn't
like her to miss school, even when she's sick, so I knew
she had to be avoiding me.

My ex-best friend, Brayden, was there though.
Since there weren't assigned seats, he came early enough
to get a seat up front, far away from me. Obviously, he
was trying to avoid me as well. I don't blame him.

"Good morning, students," said Mrs. Robinson.
"TGIF, right?"

The students murmured.

"You might be too young to understand yet," she
said. "Anyway, it's Friday, and the day of Dance 'Til Ya
Drop. You'll be happy to hear that everything planned for
it has gone well, and we're bound to have a wonderful

night tonight, so I hope that you all tried your best in raising money."

I shifted in my seat, uncomfortable at the thought of Carlyle's plan to change the mascot to a buccaneer.

"Remember that the student with the most money wins the trip to Hawaii and also the chance to change the old and outdated mascot of Buchanan from a wildcat to... well, whatever they please. What kind of mascots do you think would be good for Buchanan?"

One of the students shouted an answer. "A bald eagle!"

Another student corrected him. "A bald *dude!*"

"A zombie!"

"A *bald* zombie!"

Mrs. Robinson sighed. "A bald zombie. Y'know, the other teachers said this was a bad idea, and I'm beginning to wonder if they were right."

Silently, I nodded my head agreeing with her.

"Anyway, the event is tonight. Again, if you're not staying after school to help set up the cafeteria, then you'll need to have your parents bring you in at 4:30. It'll take some time to sign in. Bring all the money you've collected, which should've been in the form of written checks. We don't want a repeat of the food drive on our hands, do we?"

She was referring to how Wyatt had stolen all the cash from the food drive.

"You'll have to fill out a form or something, and then you'll walk into the cafeteria. The event will start at five o'clock sharp, aaaaaaaand you'll all dance until you drop. At seven o'clock, the money should be counted up, and the winner will be announced at the end of the event!"

Carlyle was sure to win the event. He was going to have all the pirates give him the money that they raised, and he had enough pirates that he would probably dominate as the winner. There was always the chance that an overachiever would upset the contest, but that was doubtful.

Mrs. Robinson continued the morning announcements, but all I heard was "blah blah blah." There was far too much on my mind. My backpack was sitting next to my desk, and inside it were my ninja robes.

I decided last night that I was just going to give up. I know it sounds lame, but there wasn't much else I could do. Carlyle's threat against Zoe walking the plank… that was one thing, but after I found out that she had actually *become* a pirate? Well, that was much *much* worse.

When I first became the ninja leader, I tried to get her to join. Yes, I realize how completely two faced that sounds because I wouldn't let Brayden in automatically. But Zoe was different. She was there when the ninja clan first contacted me and even helped me join. But she told me no when I offered her a place as a ninja.

She was nice about it – she didn't poke fun at me. I think she was genuinely happy to see me become part of a group since I was the new kid at Buchanan. Plus she had a good excuse – she wanted to participate in other groups like the cheerleading squad or even the volleyball team, which is exactly why it felt like a sucker punch to see her parading around as a pirate.

So that was it. Zoe had chosen her side. Brayden betrayed me. And I lost the entire ninja clan. Some leader I was, huh? In a way, it was sort of a relief. Carlyle would win and the school would become the Buchanan Buccaneers. His vengeance would be complete by that night.

And I wouldn't have the stress of leading a group of 6th grade ninjas so I'd be able to sink back into the invisible lifestyle I'd grown accustomed to. It wasn't a big deal… at least I'd have my comic books to keep me company.

Just then, the bell rang, signaling the end of homeroom. I completely zoned out the entire time. The rest of Mrs. Robinson's announcements went right over my head.

I grabbed my bag from the floor and turned to talk to Zoe, and then I remembered she wasn't there. Being late to school was one thing, but for Zoe to miss homeroom completely was actually something to worry about.

Brayden stopped just before exiting the room. "Where's Zoe?"

I shrugged my shoulders. "I dunno. It's not like her to miss any amount of any class."

"Weird," Brayden said before he stepped out of the door.

It *was* weird. A little *too* weird. She made her choice to become a pirate, but that didn't make her any less my cousin. I decided that I should try calling her house. My locker is where I kept my cell phone, and yes, this isn't 1990 anymore – kids have cell phones stashed away in the lockers for emergencies... what, you don't?

I dialed her home phone number and leaned my head into the inside of my locker so teachers couldn't tell what I was doing. I'm sure I looked suspicious though, I mean, my entire *head* was in my locker.

Her dad picked up. "Hello?"

"Uncle John? This is Chase. Is Zoe around?"

"Chase? Hey, buddy, what's happening?"

"Oh not much. Y'know... same old, same old, talkin' on a cell phone with my head shoved into a locker."

Uncle John laughed. "Why would you be doing that? You getting picked on again? Aren't you some sort of all mighty ninja now? Zoe talks about it all the time."

"She *does?*" I asked, surprised. "I mean, is she around? She wasn't in homeroom today, and that's not really like her so I got kind of worried."

"That's awfully nice of you, but yeah, I'm afraid she's not feeling too well. She tried going to school this morning, but I told her that if she wanted to make it to the dance tonight, she'd have to stay home and rest first."

"Oh, good," I said. "So she'll be here tonight?"

"Yep."

"Can I talk to her?"

Uncle John paused. "She's actually taking a little nap on the couch, but I can tell her you called when she wakes up. How's that sound?"

"Good," I said. "No need for her to call me back though since I'm at school. My phone's in my locker so I won't be able to get to it."

"Alright. I'll let her know you called," said Uncle John. "She'll appreciate that."

Snapping my phone shut, I tossed it back onto the top shelf of my locker. At least Zoe was all right. If anything, I felt better about that. It also made what I was going to do in gym class all the more easy.

Friday. 10:45 AM. Gym class.

Not surprising to me, Carlyle wasn't in art class.
I'm sure he was probably working on the stage in the
cafeteria, building his army of pirates. Brayden was there
though. I gave him a note to hand off to his captain, and
he said he would.

Now I'm sitting in the boy's locker room, waiting
to see if Brayden actually gave Carlyle the note.

"Chase," said Carlyle's voice.

I guess Brayden did.

I turned around and faced the pirate captain. I
wasn't surprised to see Brayden standing next to him.
"You weren't in art today, Captain Carlyle."

"I had *better* things to attend to," said Carlyle.

"Skipping class is a good way to get busted."

Carlyle laughed. "Are you warning me or
something? Trying to make sure that I don't get in

trouble?"

"No," I said. I don't know why I told him that. Maybe I was just nervous, and when I'm nervous, I always talk without thinking.

Carlyle stepped forward with his hands behind his back. "Brayden gave me your note. I assume you've called this meeting here in the locker room because you're ready to admit defeat."

I said nothing.

"It's alright, lad," said Carlyle. "Even the best of us have to fail from time to time. In your case, the time just happens to be at this moment."

I took my book bag off and dropped it on the cement in front of my feet.

Carlyle snapped his fingers, and Brayden stepped forward. He marched over to my book bag and unzipped it. Then he dug his fat hot dog fingers into it and pulled my ninja robes out. Tossing them on the floor in front of the captain, he spoke. "It's all here, capt'n."

"Good," Carlyle sneered. "Then it's just about finished, isn't it, Chase?"

I couldn't look him in the eye.

Picking up my ninja robes, he turned around and started for the door. "Hope t'see you tonight, matey. It's gonna be a heckuva dance."

I fell to my knees and felt the cold cement through my blue jeans. That was that. It was over for me, but I was numb to it. I think I realized that without Zoe on my team, I just didn't care. Weird, because not caring about something felt the same way as wanting to puke.

Friday night. 4:30 PM. My dad's car.

My dad had to drop me off at the school that night. I really *wasn't* keen on going to the dance, but since it was mandatory, I didn't have a choice. I was in the front seat as Dad drove. Of course I was, what did you think? That I was five years old and still sitting in a baby seat in the back? No way. I'm almost *twelve!*

I pushed my hand into the front pocket of my jeans and felt the skull pendant that Zoe had dropped yesterday. I brought it along so I could confront her with it.

"So you have a date for tonight?" Dad asked.

I shook my head as I stared out the window. "It's not that kind of dance."

"No? I guess I've never heard of any other kind."

"It's to raise money for cardiovascular health or whatever."

"Ah," Dad sighed. "A dance for the ol' ticker."

"And we're supposed to go until we drop."

"Drop dead?"

"Dead tired maybe. I dunno."

"Is there some sort of prize or something?"

"Yeah, but I'm pretty sure some other kid has it in the bag," I said.

"Oh, he's done more work than anyone or something?" Dad asked.

"*Something*," I repeated. "To be honest, I think that if he wins, it'll be unfair."

"Unfair? How so?"

"Well, I mean, he's only going to win because…" I trailed off. Telling my dad about the pirate invasion would've landed me in a looney bin. "Because he cheated."

Dad shook his head. "Not cool. Does anyone else know he cheated?"

"Yeah," I said. "Like, *everyone* does. Everyone except the teachers."

Dad paused. "Want me to say something to them?"

"No!" I said quickly.

Dad nodded. He was good at understanding what I felt when I didn't come out and say it. "So… what do you think you're gonna do about it?"

I pulled my foot up and rested it on the dashboard. "I thought maybe something, but what's the point? What's it worth to say anything when everyone knows anyways and actually *wants* him to win?"

The car ride was silent for a moment as Dad pulled

into the school's parking lot. I could see several of the other students getting dropped off by the front doors. Many of them were dressed as pirates.

"You didn't mention it was a costume party," Dad said.

"It's not."

When Dad pulled up to the curb to drop me off, he stopped the car and put it in park. Then he turned to me and spoke in a way that almost made him seem like he had experience with this sort of thing. "Chase, listen. I know you're probably confused about this whole thing with that kid winning the prize when he shouldn't. It bums me out a little to hear you say that you probably won't do anything about it. I'm not saying you should sound the alarms or anything… but I hope you do *something*. It's never the popular thing to go against the crowd, but at least you're standing up to it. Think about it – in a world where everyone is following the same path, you're the one who's found the strength to create your own. It might seem scary at first, but trust me – you'll feel free."

Was my dad right? Was it possible that maybe, for once in my entire life, I should actually listen to his advice? Something about what he said gave me comfort. I smiled. "Yeah, good thing I'm already pretty unpopular."

"Look at it this way," Dad said. "It might feel like the world is against you, but it's really *not* that."

"Then what is it?"

"It's that nobody is exactly *with* you," he said.

"There's a huge difference there that should give you strength."

Sometimes my dad made too much sense. "Whatever," I said with a half smile. He knew I understood.

Dad laughed and rubbed my head in a way he knew I hated. "Now get outta my car. Text me when it's almost over and I'll come back out... *maybe*."

I mocked a laugh at him as I stepped onto the curb with my yellow envelope of fundraiser money. "Har har."

As he pulled away, I turned to face Buchanan School. The whole front entrance was packed with kids talking and joking around. I couldn't see Zoe anywhere yet, but her dad said that she'd be here.

Shouts of pirate insults drifted through the air toward me, and I remembered that Monday in homeroom of how irritated it made me. Seriously, I *hate* when people talk like pirates.

Friday. 4:40 PM. Buchanan School lobby.

I waited my turn in line among a sea of costumed children. To be honest, I can understand why some kids would get so into it. They get to come to school dressed in baggy clothing that look like pajamas *and* they don't have to worry about their grammar – it *does* sound appealing. But was it necessary for many of them to stop bathing altogether? The lobby of the school stunk like moldy cheese.

"Yar, mate," said a boy in front of me. "Top of the mornin' to ya!"

"You sound like a leprechaun," I said. "Not a pirate."

"That be the best part, no?" he asked, at *least* I *think* it was a question. "We pirates live by one rule, and that's to live by *no* rules!"

My brain really felt like it was worn out from

having to translate all the jibberish coming from this kid's mouth so I had to just smile and nod at him slowly.

"Chase, your envelope please," said the teacher manning the sign-in table. It was Mr. Cooper."

I handed him my yellow envelope. As I filled out the slip of paper with my name and stuff, Mr. Cooper opened the envelope and dumped the insides out onto the table.

"You only got one check?" he asked.

"Mm-hmm," I hummed.

"And it's from your parents," he added.

"That's right," I said.

Mr. Cooper sighed. "Well, at least it's more than the other kids so far."

"What do you mean?"

The coached leaned across the table and spoke under his voice. "Nobody else raised a single penny. They've all handed in *empty* envelopes. It's rather disappointing to say the least."

I didn't speak. Mr. Cooper thought nobody raised any money, but I knew the truth. Everyone had already given Carlyle their earnings so he could win the prize. Biting my lip, I said, "Weird."

"It is," Mr. Cooper said as he took the sheet of paper with my name on it. Then he pointed at the cafeteria doors. "Welcome to the party."

The inside of the cafeteria was dark. The staff had blocked the windows with large dividers so that the disco lights near the ceiling could do their job. There was a blaze of blue and pink colors dancing on the walls as loud bass music shook the ground. When I opened the door, it was like walking into a wall of hot air. A wall of hot air that *stunk*.

Mrs. Robinson was standing just inside the door. She was holding a napkin in one hand and a half eaten cookie in the other while she moved her body slightly to the deafeningly loud music.

When she saw me, she laughed as if I caught her doing something she wasn't supposed to be doing. "Hi, Chase!" she said loudly. "Cookies and punch are on the table in the back of the room."

"Thanks!" I replied. I had no intention of actually dancing so I was happy to hear there was a table I could hang around.

As I made my way across the cafeteria, I could see that almost everyone was here already. A lot of the kids must have stayed after school to help set up the room. The most discouraging part about it was that *every single kid* was dressed as a pirate except for me. If that didn't make me stick out like a sore thumb, I don't know what else would.

I recognized a couple of the pirates. They used to be part of my ninja clan. When I made eye contact though, they looked away. Maybe *they* were embarrassed, but I couldn't help but feel like they were disappointed in me.

Zoe was supposed to be at the dance, but I still hadn't seen her at this point. I had no idea what I would say to her if I saw her, but I knew it wasn't going to be nice things.

Finally, I reached the table of cookies and punch. Kids in dumb looking pirate costumes were huddled around it, munching on fat chocolate chip cookies and spilling red juice all over the floor. There was no way I was going to push through the crowd of pirate kids so I took a spot on the wall, leaning against it. I did this for about forty-five minutes, watching carefully for any signs of Zoe.

Friday. 5:30 PM. Dance 'Til Ya Drop.

At this point in the dance, it just felt like I was at someone's Halloween party, except I was the only one who didn't get the memo that it had a pirate theme.

Carlyle had arrived and was out in the middle of the dance floor. Say what you want about the kid, but he was definitely a charmer. Girls were lined up for a turn to dance with their captain.

"Pretty gross, isn't it?" said a voice from right next to me.

I turned to face the kid. I was surprised to see it was Zoe, dressed in silly looking pirate costume. "You've got a lot of nerve," I said.

Zoe looked confused. "Huh? What're you *talking* about?"

I shook my head. "Look at what you're wearing! You've chosen which side you want to be on! Just like

Brayden and everyone else in this school! You're such a sheep."

"A sheep?" she said, upset. "How am I a sheep?"

"You're following the crowd without using your brain!" I explained. "You're not even *thinking* straight right now. I *know* it was you I was chasing yesterday."

"Chase, you'd better hang onto that tongue of yours," she sneered. "I think it's running pretty wild right now."

"We're *family!* Family is supposed to stick together, but you abandoned me!" I started laughing in a way that felt like I was a villain. "I offered you a spot in my ninja clan, and you refused because you were too cool for it! No thanks, you said! I'd like to spend my time playing volleyball and cheering for the football team, you said! But look at you now! Dressed like a frumpy pirate lost in the crowd!"

Zoe didn't say anything, but I could see that she was really angry. So angry that it looked like tears were forming in her eyes. Wait... do tears form when people get mad?

I started talking again, but she turned and walked away before I could get the words out. "I'm sor—"

"Nice," said one of the pirates who overheard our conversation. When I looked, I saw that the entire crowd of pirates around me had heard the whole thing.

Carlyle stepped forward. "Seems as though you do quite good at destroying *yourself*."

I didn't speak. The music thumped and trembled the

76

floor of the cafeteria as pirates circled around me. I've read a lot about situations like this in ninja training. When surrounded by a group of attackers… it's best to get yourself out of there. Pretty obvious, right?

"Tonight, you'll bear witness to my victory," Carlyle said as he gestured for his minions to close in and tighten their circle. He knew I was trying to get out of it.

"These kids have a right to know your intentions," I said.

The captain laughed loudly. "They already *do!* That's the most beautiful part! They *want* to help me win!"

"You want to be led by a maniac?" I asked the crowd. "You want this kid to win the prize *just* because he's a smooth talker?"

Many of the students nodded. I could see they wouldn't be convinced easily.

"What's your end-game here, mate?" Carlyle asked. "What d'you think you'll accomplish right now? The entire school be against ya!"

"It's not that anyone is *against* me," I said.

Was I really about to quote my dad?

"It's just that nobody is exactly *with* me."

Yep. I just quoted my dad.

The music playing in the background suddenly scratched to a stop, and then a girl's voice shouted from somewhere in the cafeteria. "*I'm* with you!"

At that moment, the curtain to the stage started peeling open, revealing all the work that the pirates had done that week. The Buchanan Buccaneers flag was pinned to the back wall. In front of that was a medium sized, crudely created boat that was probably supposed to be a pirate ship. At the side of the stage stood Zoe, hanging onto the rope that drew open the curtain. Many of the pirates gasped, in awe of the ship.

I didn't know what to say.

"What's the point of exposing this?" Carlyle asked. "These kids already know what the plan is!"

Zoe ran to the front of the stage and spoke to the crowd of listening students. "Do you really know what this will do to Buchanan if he changes our mascot from the Wildcats to the Buccaneers?"

There were some murmurs throughout the crowd.

"I think they do," Carlyle shouted. "Doesn't seem like they mind much either."

"You're just giving power to a different kind of bully!" Zoe said. "His intentions aren't just to win this thing."

This was when Carlyle started to grow angry. He started walking toward the stage. "You'll hold your tongue if ya know what's good for ya, lassie!"

Zoe folded her arms. "I'll do no such thing. This boy is the cousin of Wyatt! Changing the mascot to the Buccaneers is his own weird way of taking over Buchanan! It's his plan to rule over it as the pirate captain! Is this really the kid you want choosing our new mascot?"

"I said hold your tongue, or you're gonna be very sorry!" Carlyle shouted, now running full speed toward the stage.

But many of the students didn't move for him. They stood their ground, blocking him from my cousin.

"Is what she's sayin' true?" asked one of the girl pirates. "Are you really Wyatt's cousin? Is this all just some kind of revenge game for you?"

"I needn't answer to a scallywag like you!" Carlyle said. "It doesn't matter anyhow, I'm already the *winner* of the contest, and in a little bit, you'll see that my plan has become complete!"

I ran to the stage. "Zoe," I said. "But you... I thought..."

Zoe tightened the side of her mouth and shook her head at me. "You numbskull... don't you remember what I said last Monday?"

I thought as hard as I could, but couldn't recall. I shook my head.

"I said I've always got your back... no matter what. Even if it means going deep undercover."

I glanced at her pirate uniform. Then I pulled the skull pendant from my pocket. "You were undercover as a pirate?"

A smile beamed across her face as she nodded her head at me. She really *was* the coolest cousin in the world. "Yesterday, I ran from you because if any of these pirates saw us talking, my cover would've been blown. I joined the pirates to see for myself what they were doing."

"So this morning," I said. "You weren't skipping school to avoid me?"

Zoe nodded. "Oh yeah, I totally skipped to avoid you. I'm terrible at lying and I knew if you confronted me about it, I would've caved."

"I feel like an idiot," I said to her.

"Ya look like one too, matey!" Carlyle shouted. "None of this changes the fact that you're all finished! The school is mine, and Wyatt's revenge is complete! When he *returns* to this school, it'll be *ours* for the taking!"

"When he *returns* to this school?" I asked. Why would Carlyle say such a thing? Wyatt was expelled, which meant no "do-overs."

The lights in the cafeteria flickered on as some of the teachers stepped onto the dance floor. Mr. Cooper was leading the pack of adults with a stupid looking grin on his face.

"Students," he shouted loudly. "I'm sorry to interrupt…" he trailed off, confused by all the pirates standing by a stage that had a pirate ship on it. Shaking his head, he continued. "Um, weird. Anyways, I'm sorry to interrupt whatever *this* is, but it seems we have a clear winner for the event tonight."

"Keep your earballs peeled, boy," Carlyle sneered at me.

Mr. Cooper extended his arm and pointed straight at the pirate captain. "*Carlyle* has won the prize. He raised the most money out of all the entries tonight!"

Zoe jumped down from the stage. "How much did he win by? What were the totals?"

Mr. Cooper laughed. "Normally we wouldn't give out that information, but in this case, I think it's alright. There were only two students who actually raised any money at all." The coach pointed at me. "Chase collected exactly five dollars."

"And how much did Carlyle raise?" Zoe asked.

"Eleven thousand, two hundred twenty two dollars, and fifty cents," Mr. Cooper said.

"Serious?" Zoe shouted. "That doesn't seem a little strange to you?"

Mr. Cooper put his hand on his hip and crinkled his brow, thinking for a moment. Finally, he answered. "No. Not at all."

Carlyle punched me in the chest. Probably a victory punch. It wasn't hard, but it hurt. "Game over! You lost, Chase! You've lost *everything!* Your friends! Your ninja clan! Your school! Just wait until Wyatt hears about this!"

My head started spinning again. The room became a blur of bright colors and faces as Carlyle continued to celebrate his victory by jumping up and down and laughing. Zoe was off to the side, walking toward me.

"You can't let it end like this! You can't!" she said.

"What can I do?" I asked, trying to keep from falling over. My knees felt weak.

"Anything! You can't let this psychopath change the mascot! Do something! Anything!"

Some of the students behind me put their hands on my shoulder. I heard some familiar voices of my ninja clan.

"Master," a boy said. "You mustn't give in!"

Another voice spoke. "Please, we've made a terrible mistake. We let our boredom get to us! Our need for excitement blinded us!"

"But I failed you as a leader," I whispered.

One of the girls stood in front of me and looked me in the eye. "No," she said. "You were a better leader than we knew. Look at you. You're the *only one* in this gym that's not dressed as a pirate!"

"I'm *undercover*," Zoe snipped.

The same boy that talked to me after my fight with Wyatt spoke. "It's the same as before. You stood your ground and made the choice to do good. And for that alone, you deserve to be the leader."

"I don't have my ninja robe anymore," I said.

The boy tapped at my chest. "But you're a ninja in here. Besides, those robes are cheap. We have tons of extras that haven't even been opened yet. Just take one of those during the next meeting."

Suddenly, Zoe slapped my face.

"Hey!" I said as I clutched my cheek.

"You're a ninja again! Now quit feeling sorry for yourself and get our school back!" shouted my cousin.

The members of my ninja clan punched their open palms and bowed to me. The room suddenly stopped spinning, and my heart started racing. I jumped to my feet and stared at Carlyle. He was still doing his victory dance. "Hey!"

Carlyle turned to face me. "What is it, loser?"

"You won this event by cheating!" I said. "And I demand a rematch!"

"What?" Carlyle asked. "Is someone a sore loser?"

"No," I said. "I'm not. I just know that you'd lose in a match against me."

"What kind of match?" Carlyle asked, interested. "I've already won. Tell me why I'd want to keep playing with a mouse like you?"

"Because you can't *stop* yourself," I said, narrowing my eyes. "Victory tastes too sweet for you to *not* risk everything you've already achieved."

Carlyle stepped forward, silent for a second. "What be the stakes, matey?"

"You can have your trip to Hawaii," I said. "But if I win, then you give me the power to change the school's mascot."

The captain tapped at his chin. "And if you lose?"

"I'll switch schools," I said.

Zoe and my ninja clan gasped.

"Tell me that wouldn't be the greatest revenge," I said, looking directly into the eyes of the captain. "You take my friends, my ninja clan, and my school plus...*plus* I never return to Buchanan."

Carlyle laughed out loud. He looked at Mr. Cooper the way a dog does when they want to go outside.

The coach lifted his hand and waved. "I'll allow it."

"Good," I said. "Meet me at the Norwegian obstacle course in five minutes."

Friday. Five minutes later. Norwegian obstacle course.

The entire school followed us down to the track where the obstacle course was set up. Most of the students had removed their pirate costumes, but a few stragglers remained confident that Carlyle would win.

"Are you sure you know what you're doing?" Zoe asked.

I shook my head as I approached the starting line. "Nope."

"You fell off the second obstacle last time," said a voice.

I turned around and was met by Brayden. He wasn't wearing his pirate hat anymore. "Man, I'm sorry about what I did to you."

I didn't speak.

"I let it all go to my head," he said. "You didn't let me join your ninja clan, and Carlyle said I could be a pirate if I wanted to. I just… I guess I chose poorly."

"I *should've* let you in," I said. "It was dumb of me not to. I just wasn't sure of what kind of leader I could be, and I made some poor decisions."

"You seem to be doing just fine as a leader right now," he said, smirking.

"We'll see," I said. "If I lose, then everything is still under Carlyle's control."

"At this point, I think everyone has seen that you've stood against him," Brayden said. "That's a sure sign that your leadership skills can pay some bills, y'know?"

I raised my fist to Brayden, and he bumped it with his own. That was the guy way of saying things were cool.

"Wait," I said as I looked at Zoe. "If Zoe was *already* a pirate, then what was all the talk about making Zoe walk the plank?"

"*You were gonna make me walk to the plank?*" Zoe asked, angry.

Brayden put his hands up in surrender and shook his head. "No! No no no, that was all just a bluff. We knew you had no idea she was a pirate so the bluff sorta worked."

"*Double agent pirate*," Zoe corrected.

"Quit your talking!" Carlyle shouted as he approached the starting line.

Mr. Cooper joined us. "This Norwegian monster is impossible to beat so that's not what you'll be racing for. First one that gets knocked out by it is the loser. You probably should've filled out the paper work saying you won't sue the school, but... oh well."

That helped me feel a little better. I didn't need to make it to the end. I just had to last longer than Carlyle did.

A gun popped from above as Mr. Cooper raised his arm. Apparently it was the sign to go because Carlyle had already started climbing up to the rope bridge.

"Go!" Zoe cried.

I grabbed the ropes and started climbing after Carlyle who was already several feet above me. He had even started crossing the rope path that led to the rock wall about ten feet away. I gripped tighter and started moving faster.

"You're already losing!" Carlyle shouted.

I wanted to yell back, but was too focused on not falling. As soon as I pulled myself up onto the rope path, I carefully stepped each foot over the other.

The pirate captain was already standing at the spot where I fell the first time I tried playing on this thing. It was a short hop to the rock wall from where he was standing.

He stopped long enough for me to catch up to him. "That wall looks far," I said.

"Ladies first," Carlyle replied.

I took a breath and judged the distance between the wall and the bridge. It wasn't far, but the first time I jumped last Monday, I missed the handholds. Closing my eyes, I nodded, and then jumped into the unknown.

"He jumped with his eyes closed!" shouted one of the kids from the crowd.

Suddenly I heard the entire school burst with applause as I sailed through the air. It was as if time slowed down. I heard the other students cheering me on, shouting and hollering at me. My eyes shot open, and I saw Zoe covering her face, unable to watch my jump. Brayden was frozen in time with his jaw dropped and eyes peeled wide open. I even felt like I had enough time to glance back at Carlyle. The pirate captain was angrier than I'd ever seen as he watched me reach for the handholds.

I turned back around and reached my fingers out. They grazed the handholds of the rock wall and slipped off. No, I thought. Not again! As I started slipping down, I kicked my feet out and just happened to catch one of the handholds below me. It was just enough to give me another shot at grabbing the wall with my hands.

And it worked.

I gripped tightly and pulled my body against the wall. Everybody cheered again. Everyone except for Carlyle. He was behind me hurling insults in my direction.

"Oh no you don't!" Carlyle shouted as he jumped from the rope path, flailing his arms wildly toward the wall.

I could already tell this was going to end badly.

The captain's hands landed on the wall, but couldn't find anything to grip. His body was still moving at full steam as he smashed against the surface. For a second, time stopped again, and I could see his fear when we made eye contact. Then he plummeted to the pool of water below. I heard the splash as his body hit the water.

The crowd of spectators shouted at the tops of their lungs, rejoicing in my victory over the captain. A part of me felt sorry for him, but that didn't last long.

"You rotten ninja!" Carlyle cried out, splashing in the water. "You think this is the last you've heard of me?"

I climbed down from the wall and looked at him. "The mascot is mine to change," I said coldly. "You've lost."

"I take it back!" Carlyle laughed. "This was all just a joke! Buchanan will still be called the Buccaneers!"

"I'm afraid not," said Mr. Cooper. "A deal's a deal,

and you said Chase can have the opportunity to change our mascot."

"Fool!" Carlyle shouted. "You think you've won, do you? *You think this is over?*"

I looked at the defeated pirate. "I *know* it's not."

For now, the mascot was safe, and that was enough for me to let myself feel happy. A few old members of my ninja clan approached me.

"With respect," said one of the boys. "We'd like to rejoin if you'd allow us."

I shrugged my shoulders. "I don't know how different it's going to be from the last time you guys were in it."

"We wouldn't have you change a thing," said one of the girls next to him. "You've proven *twice* that you're worthy of the calling. You stood up to Wyatt, *and* you saved our school from a pirate invasion."

"I think it's important to point out that he stood up to Carlyle too," said Brayden.

The girl nodded. "Yes. That too."

"We await your answer," the boy said.

"Of course I'll still be your leader!" I said. "Why wouldn't I be?"

Punching their palms, they bowed. And then they turned and walked away. It was weird how they did that so often.

"So are we going to be called the Buchanan Ninjas?" Zoe asked.

I shook my head. "Nah, I'm not sure what it's going

to be, but I don't think our mascot should be a ninja."

"Unicorns?" Zoe suggested.

I laughed so loud that I snorted. Brayden and Zoe made fun of me, playfully punching at my arm as they did. The rest of the students had started walking back to the school, and Mr. Cooper was probably back in his office by then.

I turned back to see what Carlyle was doing, but when I looked, he was gone. Disappeared without a trace. Well, I'm sure there was some type of trace, but I didn't care enough to search.

"Go on, guys," I said. "I'll catch up."

I let Zoe and Brayden walk ahead of me as I

glanced back at the sun setting in the sky. It had been a crazy week, but at the end of it, I wouldn't have it any other way. I was still the leader of the ninja clan, which I was grateful for, but at that moment, I swore to work harder at the job. If there was any truth to what Carlyle had said – that Wyatt was returning to this school – I knew we had to be ready.

I've only been at Buchanan for a month, but I've already defeated two bullies and prevented an all out pirate invasion. There are still eight months of sixth grade left…

…I wonder what other adventures I'll have while I'm here.

Stories – what an incredible way to open one's mind to a fantastic world of adventure. It's my hope that this story has inspired you in some way, lighting a fire that maybe you didn't know you had. Keep that flame burning no matter what. It represents your sense of adventure and creativity, and that's something nobody can take from you. Thanks for reading! If you enjoyed this book, I ask that you help spread the word by sharing it or leaving an honest review!

- Marcus
m@MarcusEmerson.com

CHECK OUT THE OTHER
6th GRADE NINJA BOOKS
BY MARCUS EMERSON!

Marcus Emerson is the author of several highly imaginative children's books including the 6th Grade Ninja series, the Secret Agent 6th Grader series, and Totes Sweet Hero. His goal is to create children's books that are engaging, funny, and inspirational for kids of all ages - even the adults who secretly never grew up.

Marcus Emerson is currently having the time of his life with his beautiful wife and their three amazing children. He still dreams of becoming an astronaut someday and walking on Mars.

25364250R10065

Made in the USA
San Bernardino, CA
27 October 2015